Panda's Band

Written and illustrated by
Laura Hambleton

Collins

Panda hits the drums. He is fast.

Panda can rock! But Panda is sad.

Bat can hum.

Duck can pluck.

Rat can tap a bell.

Frog is not in luck.
He cannot hum.

Frog cannot pluck. He cannot tap.

But Panda gets Frog to hop and clap.

Frog is in the band!

Panda's band rocks!
The fans clap!

Panda's band is a big hit.

Panda's band

Ideas for reading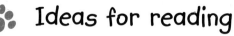

Written by Clare Dowdall BA(Ed), MA(Ed)
Lecturer and Primary Literacy Consultant

Learning objectives: read simple words by sounding out and blending the phonemes all through the word from left to right; read a range of familiar and common words and simple sentences independently; use language to imagine and recreate roles and experiences; show an understanding of the elements of stories, such as main character, sequence of events, and openings; retell narratives in the correct sequence, drawing on the language patterns of stories

Curriculum links: Creative development: Creating music and dance

Focus phonemes: r, ck, b, u, h, f, ll

Fast words: the, he, I, to

Word count: 76

Getting started

- Read the title together. Add sound buttons and practise blending the sounds to read *Panda's Band*.

- Write the word *cannot* on the whiteboard. Notice that it is made up of the two words *can/not* and practise reading it.

- Look at the focus phonemes *ck* and *ll*. Ask children to suggest words that contain these phonemes and model writing them.

- Read the blurb on the back cover together. Ask children to discuss what will happen in the story. Do they think Panda will be able to get a band?

Reading and responding

- Read pp2–3 together. Notice the exclamation mark and discuss how it affects expression.

- Ask children to explain what "Panda can rock!" means, and to suggest why he is sad.

- Support children to identify words containing the focus phonemes and practise blending to read the word, e.g. pluck and hit.

- Ask the children to read the book aloud from the beginning to the end, taking time to look at the pictures, and sounding out and blending to read new words.